The Pig Who Loved Gluffles

Loved Gluffles

And One More Story

THE PIG WHO LOVED GLUFFLES
And One More Story / by Tony Philips

ISBN 978-1-7375556-4-3 (hardcover)
ISBN 978-1-7375556-5-0 (paperback)
ISBN 978-1-7375556-6-7 (kindle)

Library of Congress Control Number: 2022917808

Idle Brains Publishing
Chicago, IL

The Pig Who Loved Gluffles
And One More Story

By Tony Philips

Idle Brains Publishing

There once was a pig who was gaga for gluffles.
He could never get enough.
One day he met a resourceful rabbit
Who sold him ten pounds of the stuff.

The pig munched it all in just one sitting
Then begged the rabbit for more.
The rabbit was startled to see the pig again
Standing outside his door.

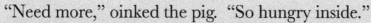

"Need more," oinked the pig. "So hungry inside."
"There's a hole in me that's burning."
"You should see a doctor," quipped the rabbit.
"You're a little crazy. It's four o'clock in the morning."

"Have more for me?" demanded the pig.
But the hare said, "Not one crumb.
I'll search around, but they're getting scarce."
So the pig waddled off looking glum.

Then the crafty rabbit crept to his secret place
Deep in the heart of the woods
Where the briars and thorns and the mud and the mulch
Hid the last of the gluffle trees' goods.

On the back of one branch on the back of one tree
Was where the gluffles grew.
It was the only place in the world, he thought,
Where there still might be a few.

So he looked and he looked and he looked some more
But there wasn't a gluffle to nuzzle.
It was as if someone had plucked them all
And guzzled them down their muzzle.

Then a rustling bush startled the rabbit
And the pig burst forth into view
He had followed the rabbit through the briars and woods
As pesky swine will do.

"What are you doing here?" snapped the rabbit, unhappy to know
The swine could find this place.
"Need more," demanded the glutinous pig
With a hungry look on his face.

Then a squeaky sneeze wafted down
From the tops of one of the trees
And clinging to a branch three hundred feet up
Was a gluffle where it shouldn't be.

"Up there?" asked the pig.
"Up there," said the rabbit, and pushed him up there so.
But pigs aren't climbers, they don't do up
Up is not their way to go.

But the smell of that gluffle wafted down
And tickled the hungry pig's snout.
As he climbed that tree, branch after branch,
He started to figure it out.

When the pig reached the gluffle, he saw it was sobbing
It was huffing and snuffling so.
"I'm the last of my kind," it gasped between sobs.
"Please don't take me, I don't want to go!"

But the pig couldn't be bothered, he was much too hungry.
"I'm sorry, I needs to eat."
"If you do," said the gluffle, "there'll be no more gluffles.
No more snacks, no more gluffle treats."

"No more gluffles?" stammered the pig. It sounded absurd.
He couldn't imagine such a place.
"I'm the last one," sobbed the gluffle. "Not one more.
You better think before you feed your face!"

So, the pig had to think, and he had to think hard.
But his brain was all mush and ice cream.
So he reached for that gluffle and started to pull
And the gluffle let out a loud SCREEEE-EAM.

Then the pig heard something that made him stop.
They say it was just one word.
They say the word he heard was "Tomorrow."
It was the call of the Tomorrow Bird.

Whatever it was, it made the pig think
Of foods he loved to eat
Like gluffle stew and gluffle toast
And gluffle salad and gluffle treats.

And the pig realized a world without gluffles
Wasn't a place he wanted to be.
And he realized he needed to change a few things.
And the first thing to change was HE.

It was at that moment they heard a crack
As the branch suddenly snapped in two
And the pig and the gluffle tumbled down
As gluffles are apt to do.

They landed on the rabbit, who broke their fall,
And smushed him to the ground.
"What took you so long?" the rabbit asked.
"Had to think," said the pig, upside down.

Then the pig plucked that gluffle off the branch
And pressed him on the tree
And the gluffle snuggled into that place –
Exactly where it wanted to be.

Now there's lots of gluffles as everyone knows.
And plenty in that particular grove.
Because the pig and the rabbit made a pact that day.
So there's gluffles tomorrow in troves.

So when you're eating your gluffles, remember the word
That made the pig pause and wait
Because sometimes it's better to think of tomorrow,
If you want gluffles on your dinner plate.

The Day We Saved the Eggs

Way back when, a long time ago,
When wacky birds ruled in the land of the snow,
On one spring day, we all came to know
There was something wrong with the eggs that we grow.

So we searched and we sought and we looked and we found
What was wrong with the eggs, it seemed, all around
Twas a tortoise, we learned, who was chomping in fury
Our beautiful eggs, which was causing us worry.

So we said, hey tortoise, what are you doing?
Do you know all the troubles you've hatched with that chewing?
We'd like you to stop those things that you're doing.
Can you eat something else, like some boiled ratatouille?

But that tortoise was stubborn, he had a thick head.
He kept right on eating, despite what we said.
He just kept on munching and chomping all day
He treated our eggs like a giant buffet.

So we thought and we pondered and brooded long too
On this egg-eating brute and what we should do.
Of this tortoise who wants to munch eggs all day
Even after we said it was not okay.

So we offered him diamonds, we offered him pearls
We offered him omelets and ice cream with swirls
But nothing would sway him, nothing at all.
He just kept on munching our eggs big and small.

We were at our wit's end, when along came this bloke
A fast-talking rabbit with a hat and a cloak
Who claimed that he knew just how to stop
This tortoise's relentless egg-eating chops.

He said turtles hate red, so he sold us some mats
We wore 'em on our heads, like big saggy hats.
But that turtle didn't mind, bite after bite
In fact, he kept eating, with no end in sight.

Then the rabbit said peanut butter would do the trick
So he mixed up a batch and sold us it quick
And we slathered it on the house and the yard to see
If that bothersome turtle would finally flee.

But that tortoise kept going. He didn't seem to mind.
The peanut butter in any way, shape or kind.
"That's what I thought," said the rabbit, stroking his chin
"Let's try a stick now. Please come, let's begin."

So he sold us some sticks, he had quite a few
He said if we waved them, the turtle would shoo.
So we waved those sticks, in the air with our claws
But the tortoise kept munching, with nary a pause.

Then the rabbit said, "We'll scare him, I know what you need,"
And he sold us some masks super ugly indeed.
But the tortoise didn't notice, he plodded along,
Not a care in the world, even humming a song.

Then the rabbit said, "A smell! Hey, a smell he don't like!
We'll make a bad smell and he'll go take a hike!"
So we sprayed all the eggs with skunk juice and squid ink.
But the turtle didn't notice, not even a blink.

Then the rabbit said, "Hey, there's this thing we can try…"
But the others said "NO!" They stopped trusting that guy
They were tired of the rabbit, whose ideas didn't work.
They were starting to think he was some kind of jerk.

Then the youngest among us, to rest, took a seat
And he sat on the tortoise, and the turtle couldn't eat!
He was stuck in his place, he was pinned like a bug.
We all wanted to give that cute baby a hug.

Then some others of us pinned the turtle down too.
And the turtle made a groan, but what could he do?
He couldn't eat our eggs, not even a munch.
Twas the end, it seemed, of his ceaseless lunch.

So it seemed we had solved this big stinking mess
But we couldn't sit on the turtle all day, I confess.
We had eggs to stack and fish to fry
And that made us sad and we let out a sigh.

Then that young'un among us started a fuss,
And he took all that junk that the rabbit sold us,
The sticks and the mats and the peanut butter too,
And he fenced in that turtle. Well, howdy do-do!

And it worked! It worked! It worked, so it seemed.
The turtle couldn't feast on our eggs that were green
There were great hurrahs and much ballyhoo
It was solved by a kid, who knew? But woohoo!

Then the rabbit, who was living on top of the hill
Hopped down and gave us a big whopping bill.
He said the fence was his idea from the start,
And we owed him big bucks or he'd take it apart.

So we strung up that rabbit by his ears and his nose
And tickled him mercilessly on the tips of his toes.
And that, my dear, is how this strange story goes.
If you don't like the ending, you can go blow your nose.

Also by Tony Philips

Packed with laugh-out loud poems and illustrations, Tony Philips's *What's Wrong with a Pet Dinosaur?* is guaranteed to make you split your pants laughing. Discover the secret letter that comes after Z, the bestest animal in the world, what pets do when their owners are away, and how to cope with a monster under your bed. If you want to find out how to have the very best birthday party, what is wrong with a pet dinosaur, and what to do if a vine grows out of your nose, then dive right in. But don't blame us if you fall off your sofa laughing.

About the Author

Tony Philips grew up in a suburb in Pennsylvania near a turkey farm. Every so often, frantic turkeys, escaped from the farm, would show up in his back yard, and he and his siblings would try to hide them. Have you ever tried to usher a crazed turkey behind a bush? It's not easy. He attended art classes at the Baum School of Art and got a degree in Creative Writing from Haverford College. He tried writing for television, but nobody wanted to hear his stories about freaked out turkeys. Or about how an unhinged turkey one time bit his younger brother on the toe. It's true, really. Tony lives in Chicago with his wife and daughter. His first book, *What's Wrong with a Pet Dinosaur?*, is available from booksellers everywhere. His ebook, *The Last Flower in the Flower Pot*, is available free at tonyphilips.com.

Lightning Source UK Ltd.
Milton Keynes UK
UKHW050741171122
412303UK00003B/112